CHRISTOPHER CHURCHMOUSE CLASSICS™

THE POTLUCK SUPPER

"He that is greedy of gain troubleth his own house"
—Proverbs 15:27.

WRITTEN BY BARBARA DAVOLL

Pictures by Dennis Hockerman

A Sonflower Book

VICTOR BOOKS ®

A DIVISION OF SCRIPTURE PRESS PUBLICATIONS INC.
USA CANADA ENGLAND

CHRISTOPHER CHURCHMOUSE CLASSICS

Saved by the Bell
The White Trail
A Sunday Surprise
The Potluck Supper
A Load of Trouble
Rainy Day Rescue

Second printing, 1988

ISBN: 0-89693-406-3

VICTOR BOOKS
A division of SP Publications, Inc.
Wheaton, IL 60187

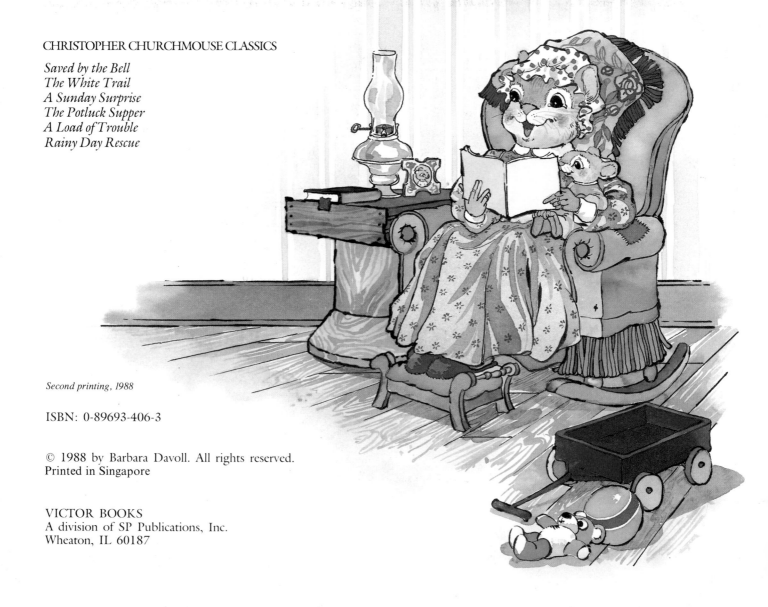

A WORD TO PARENTS AND TEACHERS

The Christopher Churchmouse Series will help children grow in their knowledge of the Lord, and at the same time bring them a delightful story about an enchanting mouse, his family, and friends.

This book, *The Potluck Supper,* one of the character-building stories in the series, is about greed. Children will learn the truth found in Proverbs 15:27: *"He that is greedy of gain troubleth his own house."* This book describes how greedy Christopher finds that the cheese he stored away makes his home a "troubled house."

Use the Discussion Starters on page 24 to help children make practical application of the biblical truth. Happy reading!

Christopher's Friend,

Barbara Davoll

Christopher Churchmouse sat up in his sardine-can bed, yawned loudly, and hopped out of bed.

All the while he was thinking, *What's so special about today?* Then he remembered. *Tonight is the potluck supper at the church!*

Christopher sighed contentedly as he thought of all the food the ladies would be bringing. *Ummm! There will probably be fried chicken and baked beans and maybe even apple pie with cheese!* He licked his whiskers and gave a happy little squeak.

4

"Time for breakfast," called Mama Churchmouse. Christopher's mama and papa were leaving that morning to visit some of Mama's sisters.

While sipping his tea Christopher thought, *I'll get some help and we'll be able to gather even more food at the potluck.* Christopher wrote his list of helpers on a chewing gum wrapper and found he had quite a crew. Then, with list in hand, he visited each of the mice. Not one refused to help. Now all he had to do was find a place big enough to store all the food.

While Christopher was thinking of the best place for the storeroom, his

5

mama came into the kitchen.

"What are you up to this morning?" asked Mama.

"Oh, nothing," replied Christopher. He thought it was best Mama and Papa didn't know his plans. Mama and Papa were always careful to take only leftovers from the church kitchen. They never touched any food until the people had eaten all they wanted.

"Papa and I are leaving now, Christopher," said Mama, giving him a hug and a kiss. "You be a good little mouse, and obey Grandpa Churchmouse. We'll be back tomorrow."

When Mama and Papa had gone, Christopher thought again of his plan to get food. He wished he could store all the food close to his own home. Then he could get to it more 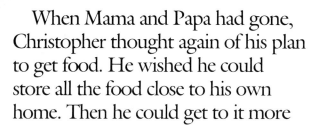 easily than the other mice. He planned to work harder than the others, so why shouldn't the food be closer to him? He thought of an old store-room next to his bedroom. He could make it bigger while Mama was away, and she wouldn't know about it.

That afternoon Christopher finished making the storage room bigger in time to scurry downstairs and watch the ladies arrive with their food.

Oh, my! The smells were enough to drive a mouse wild! From his lookout on top of the piano, Christopher wondered if the people would ever stop eating. Finally the pianist started playing.

With a big jump, Christopher
scurried down the back of the piano
and across the floor into the kitchen.
Giving a shrill little shriek, which was
the signal for his helpers to come, he
began to squeak orders.

"Hurry, fellas! Their program will
only be an hour. They'll soon be com-
ing to clean up the kitchen. Hurry!
Grab that chicken leg and pie!"

Soon all was moving smoothly
and Christopher looked around to see
what he could take. Then he saw the
open refrigerator door! With some ef-
fort Christopher hopped up on the
cabinet and then jumped to the refrigerator door. With a big heave he
swung on the door and soon was in-
side on the bottom shelf.

What he saw made him whistle.
There was the biggest round of cheese
he had ever seen! Whew! What a
find!

Christopher tried to figure out how to break the cheese into small enough pieces to take to his store-room. Just then Grandpa Churchmouse jumped up beside him.

"Well, Chris, what are you up to?"

"Oh, hi, Grandpa! Look what I've found," squeaked Christopher. "Will you help me get this cheese home?"

Grandpa peered at him and said, "Why, Christopher! I'm surprised! You *know* that would be greedy! This isn't leftover cheese—this is a brand-new one! You know we only take leftovers."

"Oh, come on, Grandpa!" pleaded Christopher.

"Chris, my boy," said Grandpa, "we have plenty of leftovers out here. Don't be greedy!" And with that Grandpa jumped out of the refrigerator, leaving Christopher all by himself.

But Christopher wouldn't listen to Grandpa. He whistled for the others to come and help him. The other mice stopped and perked up their ears at his whistle. Just then Grandpa said, "Wait, mice! We mustn't take that cheese. It isn't left over. We've all this other food! Let's not be greedy, children!" The other mice looked up at Christopher and then back at Grandpa.

"Grandpa's right," they said, and began to carry away the crumbs of all the leftovers.

"You mice are making a mistake!" yelled Christopher. But no one was listening. So Christopher started ripping the cheese apart and carting it back in his wagon to his storeroom.

It was hard work with no help, but he managed to get almost all of the cheese stored before the program was over. This took Christopher so long that he wasn't able to get any other crumbs. But as long as he had the cheese, nothing else mattered to Christopher.

12

That night he proudly looked over his storage room almost filled with his cheese! He wouldn't have to work all winter! After a delicious midnight snack of cheese, Christopher crawled happily into bed.

I won't even have to leave my own home for food, he thought proudly to himself. *This is one time Grandpa was wrong. Everything is just fine. Mama and Papa won't even know about my cheese. I'll have it all to myself!*

The next morning Christopher woke up and realized it was winter. He knew that soon the caretaker would turn on the furnace, and then his little home would be snug and cozy. Usually he dreaded winter because it was so hard to find food. But not this winter! While the others were scrounging for food, he could play. He had plenty of cheese for the whole winter.

Later in the morning, the little Churchmouse home got warmer and warmer. Christopher curled up in a big chair to read. *And I have all my cheese too*, he thought.

In the afternoon Christopher noticed a very peculiar smell. What was it? He darted from corner to corner trying to find it. Could it be his boots? No, it was even worse. Mama and Papa were still away, so he couldn't ask them. By evening the smell was so bad Christopher could hardly stand it.

Maybe Grandpa will know, he thought, so he scurried to Grandpa's little home. He knocked loudly and heard Grandpa say, "Come in." Grandpa was sitting in his rocker, quietly rocking.

"Grandpa! Grandpa! Don't you smell it?" shouted Christopher.

"Smell what, my boy?" said Grandpa.

"The smell! That awful smell!" gasped Christopher.

"Can't say as I do, Chris."

"But, Grandpa, you *must* smell it!" Christopher said, making a terrible face. "It's awful!"

"Don't smell it in here, do you, boy?" asked Grandpa.

"Why, no, I don't," answered Chris, sniffing the air. "Come to our house, and tell me what it is!"

"I know what it is, Christopher," said Grandpa sadly.

"You do?" asked the little mouse. "I've got to find out before my parents come home."

"It's the cheese, Christopher."

"THE CHEESE?" squealed Christopher.

"Yes, the cheese. A very *bad* smelling cheese. Now that the furnace is on, the smell will get worse."

"But, Grandpa, you didn't tell me," began Christopher.

"You wouldn't listen, son. I told you not to be greedy."

"But, Grandpa! I can't stand it. What can I do?" squeaked Christopher. "Mama and Papa will be so upset."

"Yes, they will, Chris," Grandpa said sadly. "You'll have to get rid of the cheese."

"But who will help me?" asked Chris. "I can't do it alone!"

"Oh, yes, you can," said Grandpa. "You got it all by yourself, so you'll have to get rid of it by yourself."

Christopher left quietly. When he got near his home he could smell the cheese. It was even worse than before.

16

He'd have to get rid of the cheese tonight before Mama and Papa came home. So he began carting the cheese out behind the church. This work was much harder than hauling the cheese from the church kitchen. Christopher had to cart the cheese a long way from the church so the people wouldn't be bothered by the smell. The smell made him feel sick all over, so he put a clothespin on his nose, but he could still smell the cheese.

Just as Christopher was taking a wagon load through the door, Mama and Papa returned.

"Why, Christopher, why aren't you in bed?" asked Mama anxiously. "Grandpa said he would look after you for us."

"He did, Mama. He knows I'm not in bed," replied the little mouse.

"What are you doing?" demanded Papa. "And what is that smell?"

"Oh, my!" coughed Mama, wrinkling her tiny nose. "Oh, my! What is that horrible odor?"

"It's the cheese," muttered Chris.

"What cheese?" questioned Papa suspiciously. "You aren't making sense."

"This cheese," said Christopher, pointing to the wagon.

18

Papa took a pawful of cheese. Holding it to his nose, he sniffed and then threw it back in the wagon. "Whew!" he said disgustedly. "Even mice won't eat that stuff. Only humans like cheese that strong. Where did you get it, son?" Papa asked.

"From the church kitchen," answered Christopher. "I've got the storeroom next to my bedroom full of it."

"Oh, my!" Mama gasped, wiping her eyes. "You'll have to get rid of it right away," she said sternly. "I won't have that smelly stuff here."

"I know. That's what I'm doing now," Christopher squeaked miser-

20

ably, hoping his papa might help him.

"I can't believe Grandpa would let you do this," worried Papa.

"He didn't," said Chris forlornly. "He told me I was being greedy."

"And you disobeyed him, didn't you?" continued Papa solemnly.

"Yes," nodded the sad little mouse. "Oh, Papa, I thought if I got all this cheese and stored it, I wouldn't have to work. I'd be able to play."

"And you thought you'd keep it all to yourself, didn't you?" interrupted his papa gently. By now,

Christopher was in his papa's arms and Papa was wiping his tears.

"Oh, Chris, what a hard lesson to learn. You've been disobedient and very selfish and greedy. I wish I could help you take the cheese away, but I can't. You'll have to do it yourself so you will learn not to be greedy." And with that Mama and Papa went to Uncle Rootie's and left poor Christopher to get rid of the cheese.

As Christopher worked all that night to get rid of the cheese, he was learning a lesson. We can find it in the Bible: "He that is greedy of gain troubleth his own house" (Proverbs 15:27). Chris was learning a very valuable lesson that children must also learn. When we want things all for ourselves, we often end up in trouble, just like Christopher.

You can be sure Christopher was a much wiser mouse at the next potluck supper.

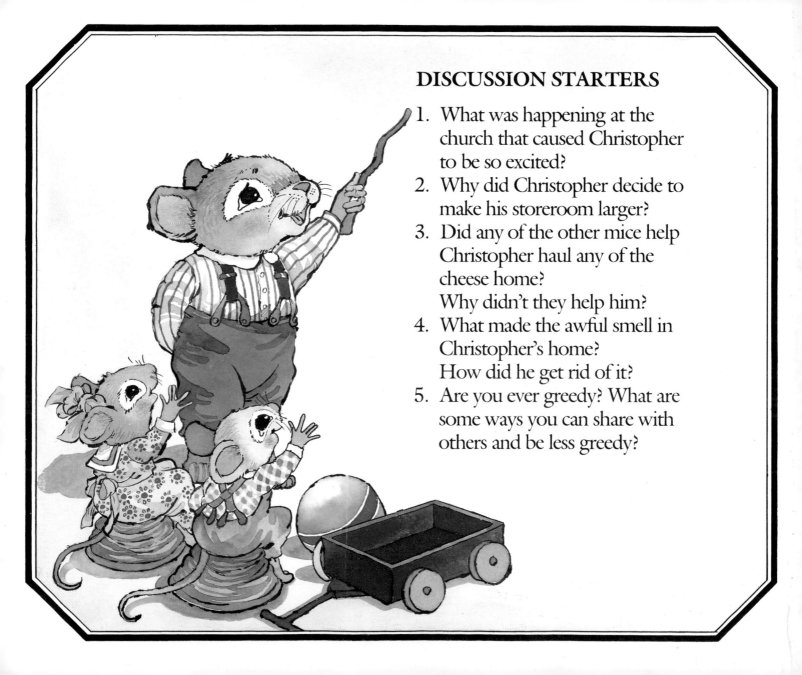

DISCUSSION STARTERS

1. What was happening at the church that caused Christopher to be so excited?
2. Why did Christopher decide to make his storeroom larger?
3. Did any of the other mice help Christopher haul any of the cheese home?
   Why didn't they help him?
4. What made the awful smell in Christopher's home?
   How did he get rid of it?
5. Are you ever greedy? What are some ways you can share with others and be less greedy?